Runaway Cakes
and Skip

Retold by *Rose Impey*

Illustrated by *Priscilla Lamont*

Other titles in this series:

Bad Bears and Good Bears
Bad Boys and Naughty Girls
Greedy Guts and Belly Busters
Hairy Toes and Scary Bones
I Spy, Pancakes and Pies
If Wishes were Fishes
Knock, Knock! Who's There?
Over the Stile and into the Sack
Silly Sons and Dozy Daughters
Sneaky Deals and Tricky Tricks
Ugly Dogs and Slimy Frogs

ORCHARD BOOKS
96 Leonard Street, London EC2A 4XD
Orchard Books Australia
14 Mars Road, Lane Cove, NSW 2066
First published in Great Britain in 2000
First paperback publication 2000
Text © Rose Impey 2000
Illustrations © Priscilla Lamont 2000
The rights of Rose Impey to be identified as the author
and Priscilla Lamont as the illustrator of this work
have been asserted by them in accordance with the
Copyright, Designs and Patents Act, 1988.
A CIP catalogue record for this book is available
from the British Library.
ISBN 1 86039 969 X (hardback)
ISBN 1 86039 970 3 (paperback)
1 3 5 7 9 10 8 6 4 2 (hardback)
1 3 5 7 9 10 8 6 4 2 (paperback)
Printed in Great Britain

★ CONTENTS ★

The Johnny-Cake

There was once an old man and an old woman and a little bright-eyed boy.

One day the old woman made
a johnny-cake for breakfast.

She put it in the oven and told
the little boy to watch the cake,
while she and the old man went
out to work in the garden.

The little boy kept his
bright eyes on the oven door
but suddenly it popped open.

Out jumped Johnny-Cake and raced across the kitchen floor.

"Come back!" called the little boy. "Cakes don't run away."

But this one did.

He rolled through the door,
along the path, out of the gate
and down the road. And the
bright-eyed boy ran after him.

"Help! Help!" he called. "The cake's run away."

The old man threw down his hoe and the old woman threw down her rake and they ran after Johnny-Cake too. But Johnny-Cake ran faster.

Soon the old man and the old woman and the bright-eyed boy had to stop for a rest.

Johnny-Cake didn't; he went on running.

By and by he came to two men digging a ditch.

"Where are you going, you crisp little cake?" they called to him.

Johnny-Cake called back,

"I've outrun the old man
and the old woman
and the bright-eyed boy.

And YOU'LL have to run fast
and stay awake,
If you want to catch up
with Johnny-Cake!"

"Oh, we will, will we?" said the men. They threw down their spades and ran after him, but they had to give up and stop for a rest too.

On and on ran Johnny-Cake. By
and by he met a big brown bear.

"Where are you going, you
jolly little cake?" growled Big
Brown Bear.

Johnny-Cake called out,

*"I've outrun the old man
and the old woman
and the bright-eyed boy
and the two ditch-diggers.*

*And YOU'LL have to run fast
and stay awake,
If you want to catch up
with Johnny-Cake!"*

"We'll see about that," growled the bear and he trotted as fast as his legs would carry him.

But it wasn't fast enough. Big Brown Bear soon gave up and lay down by the side of the road, panting.

But on and on went Johnny-Cake. By and by he met a wide-awake wolf.

"Where are you going, you crunchy little cake?" snapped Wide-Awake Wolf.

Johnny-Cake called back,

"I've outrun the old man
and the old woman
and the bright-eyed boy
and the two ditch-diggers
and Big Brown Bear.

And YOU'LL have to run fast
and stay awake,
If you want to catch up
with Johnny-Cake!"

"I *am* wide awake," said the wolf, "and I can run fast." But Wide-Awake Wolf was soon tired out and had to lie down too.

On and on went Johnny-Cake.
By and by he met Fast-Asleep Fox.

Oh, but he wasn't really fast asleep. He was just pretending. He opened one eye, then he closed it. He called out in a sleepy voice, "Where are you going, my dear, delicious Johnny-Cake?"

Johnny-Cake called out,

"I've outrun the old man
and the old woman
and the bright-eyed boy
and the two ditch-diggers
and Big Brown Bear
and Wide-Awake Wolf.

And YOU'LL have to wake up
and stay awake,
If you want to catch up
with Johnny-Cake!"

Then Not-So-Fast-Asleep Fox stretched his neck and put one paw behind his ear. He called out again in a soft voice, "I'm afraid I can't quite hear you. Perhaps you could come a little closer?"

This time Johnny-Cake stopped running.

He went back a little way and said in a much louder voice,

"I've outrun the old man
and the old woman
and the bright-eyed boy
and the two ditch-diggers
and Big Brown Bear
and Wide-Awake Wolf.

And YOU'LL have to wake up
and stay awake,
If you want to catch up
with Johnny-Cake!"

Then that cunning old fox, who was wide awake now, said in a feeble voice, "I'm sorry, I *still* can't quite hear you. Won't you come a little closer?"

Johnny-Cake came much closer
and this time he really shouted,

"*I've outrun the old man*
and the old woman
and the bright-eyed boy
and the two ditch-diggers
and Big Brown Bear
and Wide-Awake Wolf.

And YOU'LL have to wake up
and stay awake,
If you want to catch up
with Johnny-Cake,
Mr Fast-Asleep Fox!"

But now the fox was Fast-On-His-Feet Fox and he leapt up and grabbed Johnny-Cake in his sharp teeth. He threw back his head and – snip! snap! – in two big bites he swallowed him up.

That's the end;
this tale's done.
Nothing's left;
not even a crumb.

Yum! Yum! Yum!

★ The Old Iron Pot ★

There was once an old couple who
worked for a rich and greedy man.
He paid them so little they were
always hungry and at last they
had to sell their one and only cow.

The old man set off for market
and on the way he met a strange
little fellow who offered him an old
iron pot in exchange for the cow.

The old man laughed. "A pot?"
he said. "What use is a pot to me?"

Suddenly the pot gave a little skip and said, "If you don't try you won't know."

The old man could see this must
be a magic pot, so he handed
over his cow and took the pot
home with him.

"What's this?" said his wife. "We can't eat a pot and we surely have nothing to put in it."

Suddenly the pot gave another little skip and said,

"Clean me up as good as new,
Then you'll see what I can do."

The old woman took the pot and cleaned it up until she could see her face in it.

She put the pot on the shelf, but straightaway it jumped down and skipped towards the open door.

"I skip! I skip!" sang the iron pot.
"Where do you skip?" asked the old woman.

> "I skip! I run! As fast as I can,
> Off to the house of the
> very rich man."

Then the old iron pot skipped and ran down the road until it came to the house of the very rich and greedy man who lived near by.

The pot skipped into the kitchen where the cook was making a huge plum pudding. It was so huge she had no pot big enough to cook it in.

When she saw the iron pot she said, "Just what I need." And she popped the pudding into it.

But before she could put it on the fire to cook, the pot gave another skip and set off towards the door.

"Where are you going with my pudding?" called the cook.

"I skip! I run! As fast as I can,
Off to the house of the
very poor man."

The old couple were delighted when they saw what the iron pot had brought them – enough plum pudding to last them a week.

When the pot was empty the old woman cleaned and shone it and put it back on the shelf.

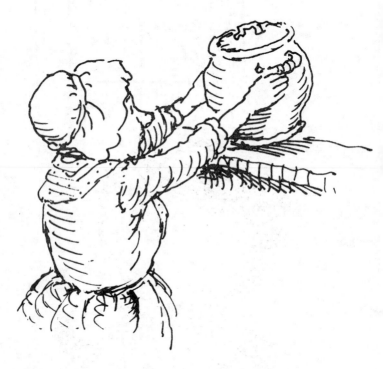

Immediately the pot jumped down and skipped out of the door.

"Where do you skip this time?"
called the old woman.

"I skip! I run! As fast as I can,
Off to the house of the
very rich man."

When the iron pot reached
the rich man's house, it skipped
straight into the room where the
rich man sat counting his money.

There was so much gold and
silver he hardly knew what to put
it in, until he saw the pot.

"Just what I need," he said.

But as soon as he'd filled the
iron pot with gold and silver it
skipped off again. The rich man
started to run after the pot, but he
couldn't catch it.

"Stop! Come back!" he shouted. "Where are you going with my money?"

"I skip! I run! As fast as I can,
Off to the house of the
very poor man."

When the old couple saw what the iron pot had brought them this time they couldn't believe their eyes. There was enough money to last them for the rest of their life.

But the pot still hadn't finished.
It tipped itself up and emptied out
every single coin, then it started to
skip again.

"Now where are you going?"
called the old woman.

"Come back," called the old
man. "We need nothing else."

But the pot kept on running,
back down the road where it met
the rich man still huffing and
puffing along.

"There you are," he panted.
"I've got you this time."

But he was wrong. The pot had got *him*. As soon as he grabbed it he couldn't let go. The iron pot and the very rich man, went skipping

and tripping

and stumbling

and tumbling

for miles
and miles.

The rich man was so out of
breath he could hardly speak.
"Slow down!" he panted.
"Where are you taking me?"

But the iron pot skipped even
faster and sang for anyone to hear,

*"I skip! I run! As fast as I can,
To the ends of the earth
with the very rich man."*

And that is just what he did.

So, unless the rich man's died,
They could still be skipping
far and wide.

There are stories about runaway cakes from many countries including *The Wonderful Cake* from Ireland, *The Wee Bannock* from Scotland, and *The Doughnut* or *The Bun* from Russia. Probably the best-known story, *The Gingerbread Man*, is American, as is *The Johnny-Cake*. *The Old Iron Pot* comes from Denmark.

Here are some more stories you might like to read:

About Runaways:

The Gingerbread Boy
from *The Orchard Book of Nursery Stories*
by Sophie Windham
(Orchard Books)

About Magic Objects:

The Magic Porridge Pot
from *The Orchard Book of Nursery Stories*
by Sophie Windham
(Orchard Books)

Tomkin and the Three Legged Stool
from *The Thistle Princess and Other Stories*
by Vivian French
(Walker Books)

A Magic Whistle
from *Myths and Fairy Tales Collection*
by Neil Philip and Nilesh Mistry
(Dorling Kindersley)